Em Majdob
Lost Days

OFFICIAL TRAILER

LitPrime Solutions
21250 Hawthorne Blvd
Suite 500, Torrance, CA 90503
www.litprime.com
Phone: 1 (209) 788-3500

Published by LitPrime Solutions   10/10/2020

ISBN: 978-1-953397-27-0(sc)
ISBN: 978-1-953397-28-7(e)

Library of Congress Control Number: 2020919921

CYBERFORCE
1
E.S
EAST SUMMET
RASTER MASTER

RASTER MASTER
E.S
EAST SUMMET

CYBERFORCE

HUFF! HUFF!
I WILL NOT STAND BY WHILE THERE ARE JERKS PICKING ON SOMEONE SMALLER THAN THEM.
WHY ARE YOU DOING THIS? YOU'RE HURT!
TCH!
I WON'T LET THEM ENJOY THIS!

LEAVE HIM BE, HOPE.
HEY CASEY, ISN'T THAT MATTEO OVER THERE.
AREN'T YOU GOING TO HELP HIM?

BUT ISN'T HE YOUR NEIGHBOR?
IT DOESN'T MATTER.
NO, HE GOT HIMSELF IN THIS, AS USUAL HE SHOULDN'T INTERFERE WITH OTHER PEOPLE'S PROBLEMS, DUMMIES NEVER LEARNS.

THANK YOU.

NO PROBLEM.

NEXT DAY...

HEY MATTEO.
OH, HEY RICKY.
HAVE YOU HEARD ABOUT THE HAUNTED HOUSE?

WHAT HAUNTED HOUSE?

THEY SAY THAT ONCE YOU ENTER IT, EITHER DAYTIME OR NIGHTTIME.
IT'LL STILL BE AS DARK AS THE DEAD OF NIGHT, THE GROUND VIBRATES HARDER AND HARDER WITH EVERY STEP IN.

SOUNDS FUN, LET'S CHECK IT OUT AFTER SCHOOL.
THAT'S WHY YOU INFORMED OF THIS, RIGHT?
HUH?
UGH, RIGHT.
UH, ME AND MY BIG MOUTH.

SO, YOU READY?
UH-HA.
MAN IT'S SO DARK IN HERE.

HOPE, DON'T WORRY WE'RE NOT STAYING THE NIGHT HERE, IT'S ALWAYS DARK IN THIS PLACE, I'M SURPRISED IT EVEN GOES THIS FAR.
CASEY, MAYBE WE SHOULD HEAD BACK, I DON'T LIKE BEING HERE.
I KNOW, BUT...
HOPE.
UGH!
NGH!

HOPE, DON'T WORRY, THIS PLACE WON'T FALL ON US, I'M SURE OF IT.
I'VE GOT A FEELING THAT SOMETHING GREAT IS GOING TO HAPPEN TO US.
HUH?
IT ALMOST FEELS NOSTALGIC DESPITE THAT IT DIDN'T HAPPEN YET.
TRUST ME ON THIS ONE.

00:05

00:03

00:02

01

FOUND ANYTHING?
NO.
HOW THE HELL DID SOMEONE FIND A WAY OUT.
IF THERE IS, LOOKS LIKE ALL THOSE RUMORS THAT WE HEARD WERE JUST RUMORS.
SIGH, OKAY LET'S GET OUTTA HERE.

NGH, MATTEO!
RICKY!
AAAAGHHH!

CASEY...
AAAAGHHH!

OOF!
WHAT IS THIS PLACE?
WHOO!

AN UNDERGROUND BASE.

THIS IS WHAT WAS CAUSING THE VIBRATIONS.

00:00

THE BASE WAS ON AN ACTIVATION COUNTDOWN.

IT MUST'VE THOUGHT THAT WE WERE ONE ... OF ITS... CREATORS OR SOMETHIN.

00:00

HELP!

BUT WHY IS IT HERE?

CASEY! WHAT'S GOING ON?
JUST SHUT UP AND FIGHT!
CASEY?

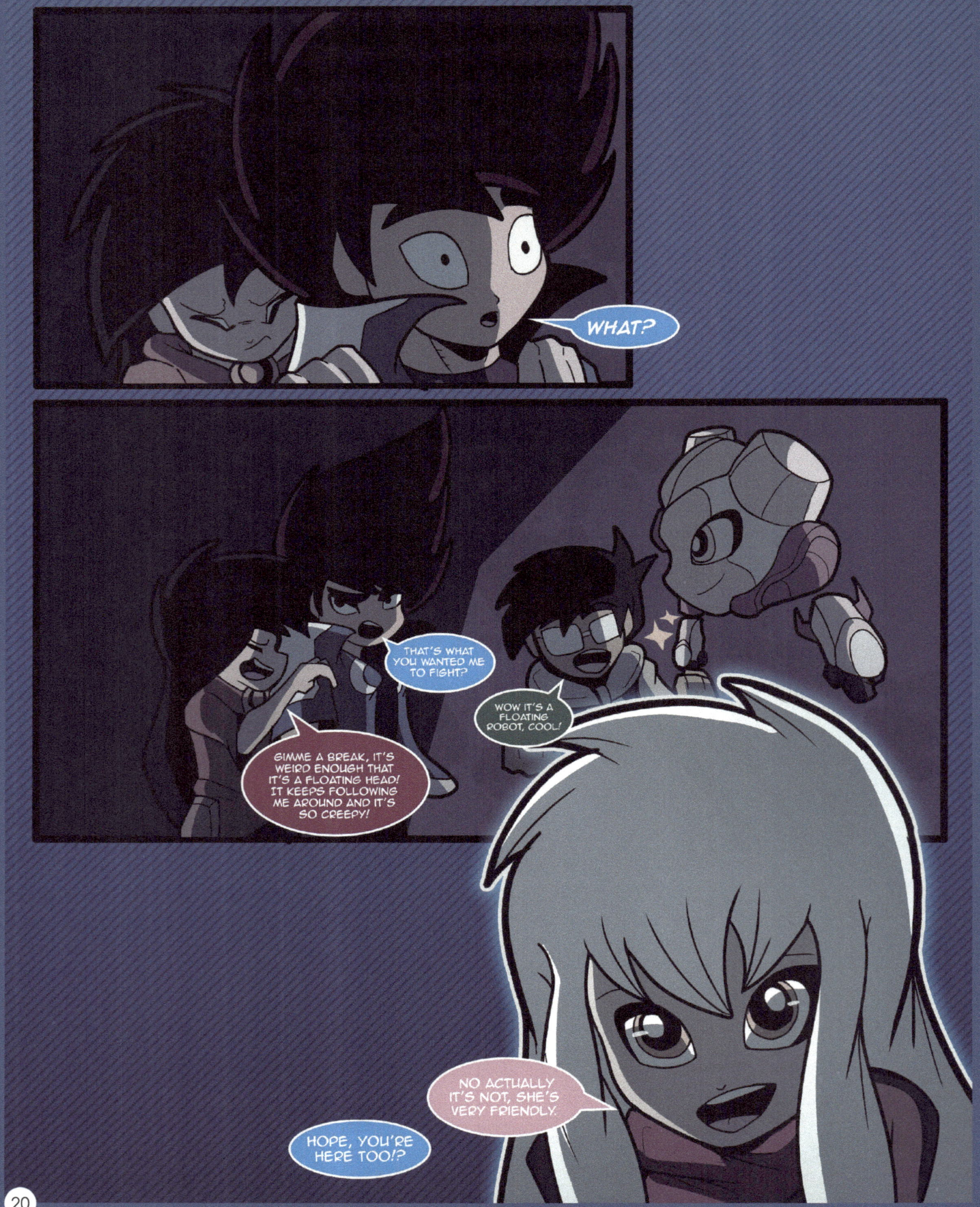

WHAT?
THAT'S WHAT YOU WANTED ME TO FIGHT?
WOW IT'S A FLOATING ROBOT, COOL!
GIMME A BREAK, IT'S WEIRD ENOUGH THAT IT'S A FLOATING HEAD! IT KEEPS FOLLOWING ME AROUND AND IT'S SO CREEPY!
NO ACTUALLY IT'S NOT, SHE'S VERY FRIENDLY.
HOPE, YOU'RE HERE TOO!?

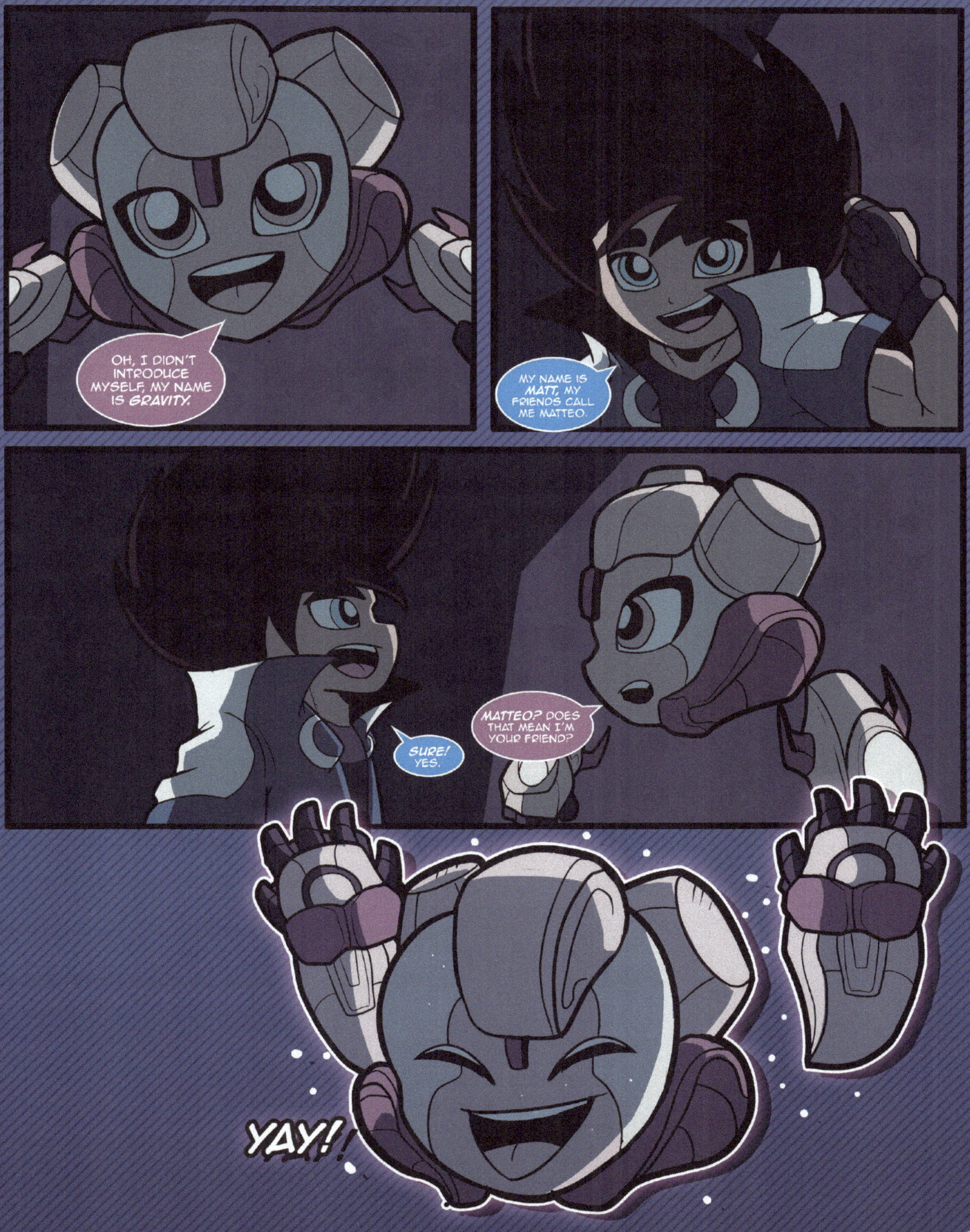

OH, I DIDN'T INTRODUCE MYSELF, MY NAME IS GRAVITY.

MY NAME IS MATT, MY FRIENDS CALL ME MATTEO.

SURE! YES.
MATTEO? DOES THAT MEAN I'M YOUR FRIEND?
YAY!

BEEP!
EEP!
EEP!
BE
WHAT'S GOING ON?
THE COMMANDER HAS BEEN AWAKENED.
PODS 01, 02 UNLOCKED,
PROTOCOL TIME-RELEASE INITIATED, POD 03, 04.
TO BE CONTINUED...

PG01

CONCEPT ART

CYBER**F**ORCE

AUTHOR'S NOTES

THIS IS MY FIRST FULL-LENGTH 20 PAGES COMIC BOOK. I PUBLISH IT ON AMAZON KINDLE AS AN EBOOK EXCLUSIVE.

PGOZ
CONCEPT ART

CYBER**F**ORCE

AUTHOR'S NOTES

THIS IS MY FIRST FULL-LENGTH 20 PAGES COMIC BOOK. I PUBLISH IT ON AMAZON KINDLE AS AN EBOOK EXCLUSIVE.

CYBER**F**ORCE

AUTHOR'S NOTES

I WAS ABOUT TO CREATE A PAPERBACK EDITION BUT GAVE UP ON THAT IDEA BECAUSE THE BOOK DIDN'T GENERATE PROFIT.

PG04

CYBERFORCE

AUTHOR'S NOTES

I WAS ABOUT TO CREATE A PAPERBACK EDITION BUT GAVE UP ON THAT IDEA BECAUSE THE BOOK DIDN'T GENERATE PROFIT.

ORIGINALLY AT THE TIME OF ITS CONCEPTION, I WAS WORKING FOR A SMALL KIDS APP DEVELOPMENT START UP COMPANY.

I WAS ABOUT TO PITCH TO THEM THE CONCEPT TO MAKE A GAME OUT OF IT, BUT THEY REJECTED IT BECAUSE IT WAS TOO AMBITIOUS.

HOPEFULLY IF THIS BOOK GETS ENOUGH LOVE.

I'LL HAPPILY START MAKING THIS GAME WITH THE FUNDING THAT THIS BOOK GENERATES.

IT WOULD MEAN THE WORLD TO ME AS THIS CONCEPT AND THIS STORY HOLDS A SPECIAL IN MY HEART.

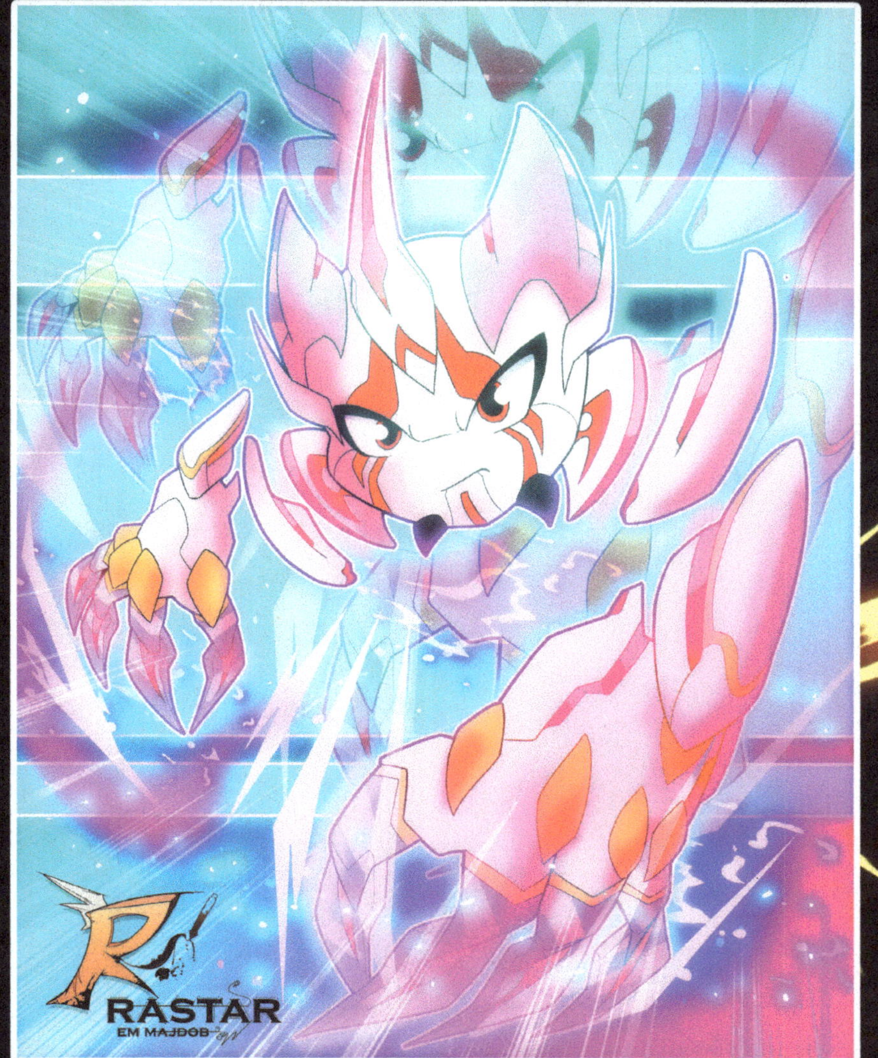

SOUNDWAVE

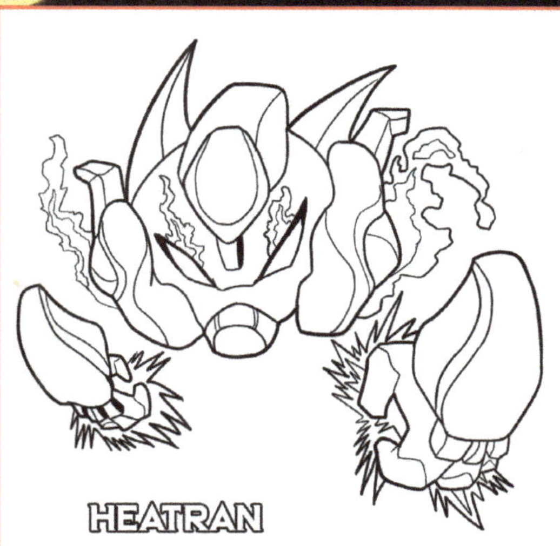
HEATRAN

HERE'S SOME CONCEPT ART OF SOME OF THE **ROBOTS** THAT ONE DAY WILL GET FEATURED

PG06

IN THIS GAME.

JIN-9

THE COMIC SERIES
WRITTEN AND ILLUSTRATED BY
EM MAJDOB

THE JOURNEY BEGINS!

EM MAJDOB

#1

NATIVE CITY
10:01 AM

MOM, DAD?

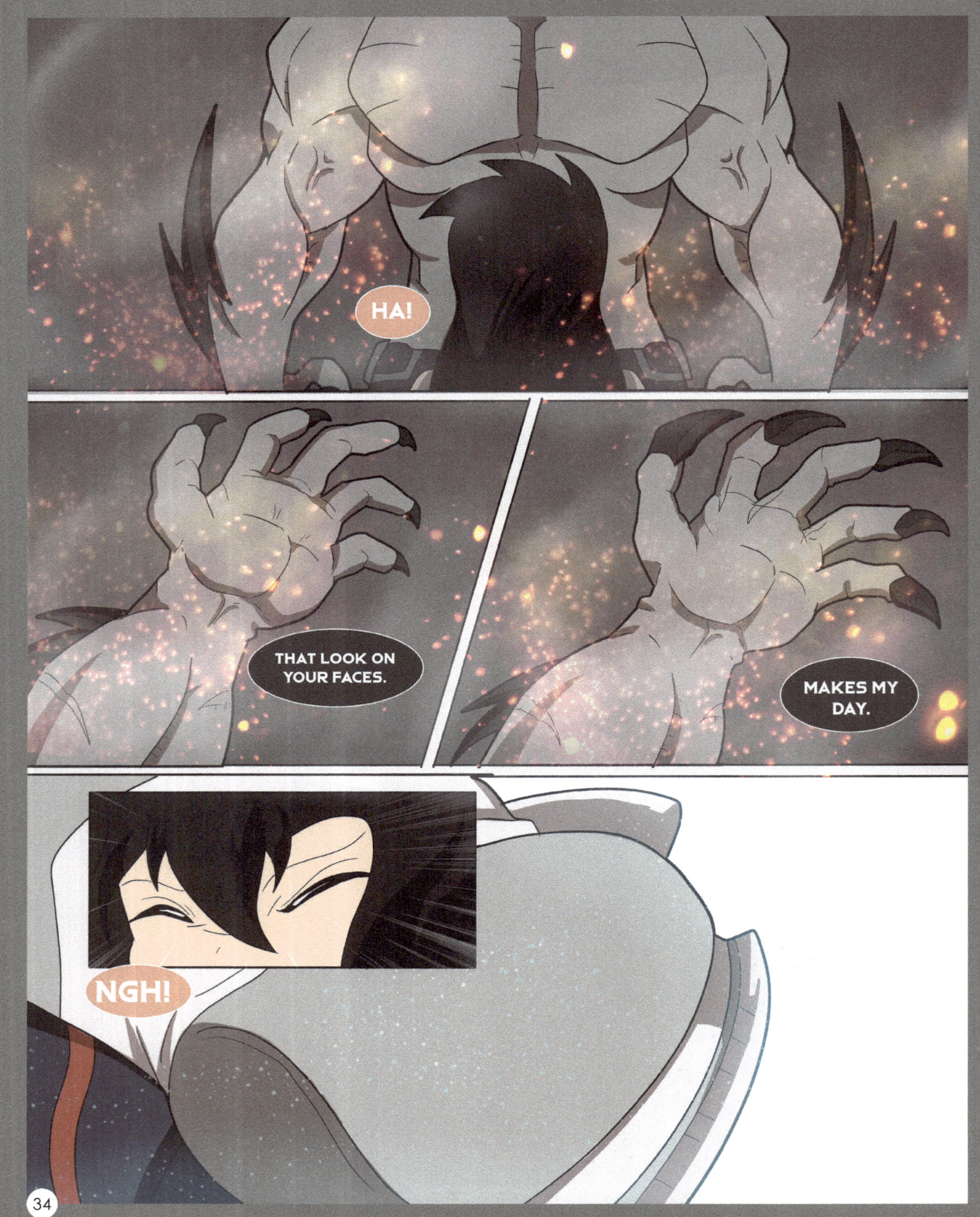

HA!
THAT LOOK ON YOUR FACES.
MAKES MY DAY.
NGH!

FINALLY I WAS WONDERING WHAT TO DO TO GET A LITTLE ATTENTION AROUND HERE?

THEN CAME IN THE BIG GUN.
LISTEN UP, BRAT!

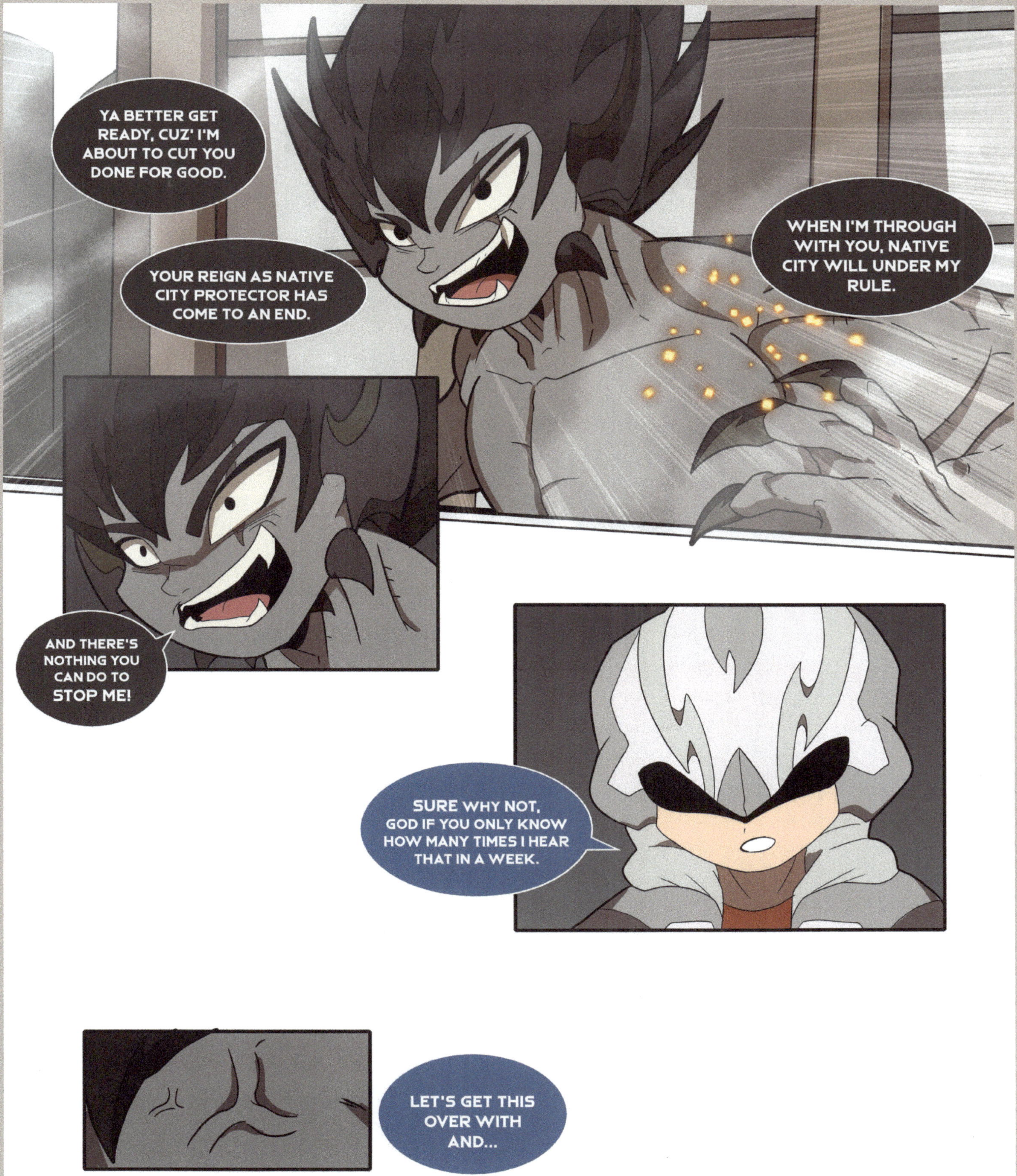

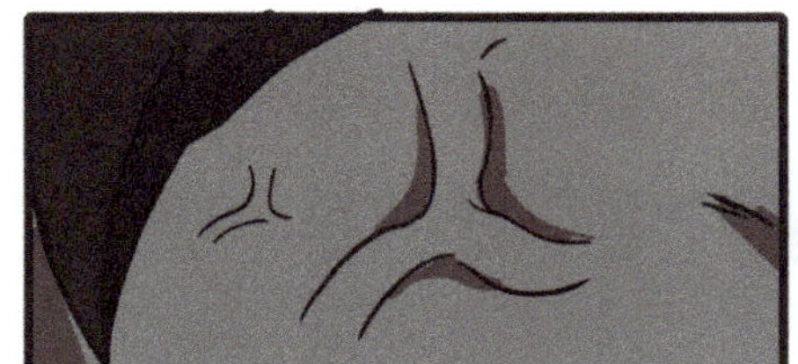

YA BETTER GET READY, CUZ' I'M ABOUT TO CUT YOU DONE FOR GOOD.
YOUR REIGN AS NATIVE CITY PROTECTOR HAS COME TO AN END.
WHEN I'M THROUGH WITH YOU, NATIVE CITY WILL UNDER MY RULE.
AND THERE'S NOTHING YOU CAN DO TO STOP ME!
SURE WHY NOT, GOD IF YOU ONLY KNOW HOW MANY TIMES I HEAR THAT IN A WEEK.
LET'S GET THIS OVER WITH AND...

YOU DARE MOCK ME!
GAAAAAGHH!

THAT'S ALL YOU'VE GOT?
AS LONG AS I'M HERE, NONE OF YOU CLOWNS WILL BE ABLE TO TAKE OVER NATIVE CITY.
SO GIVE IT UP.

YOU'RE SAFE NOW.

THANK YOU.

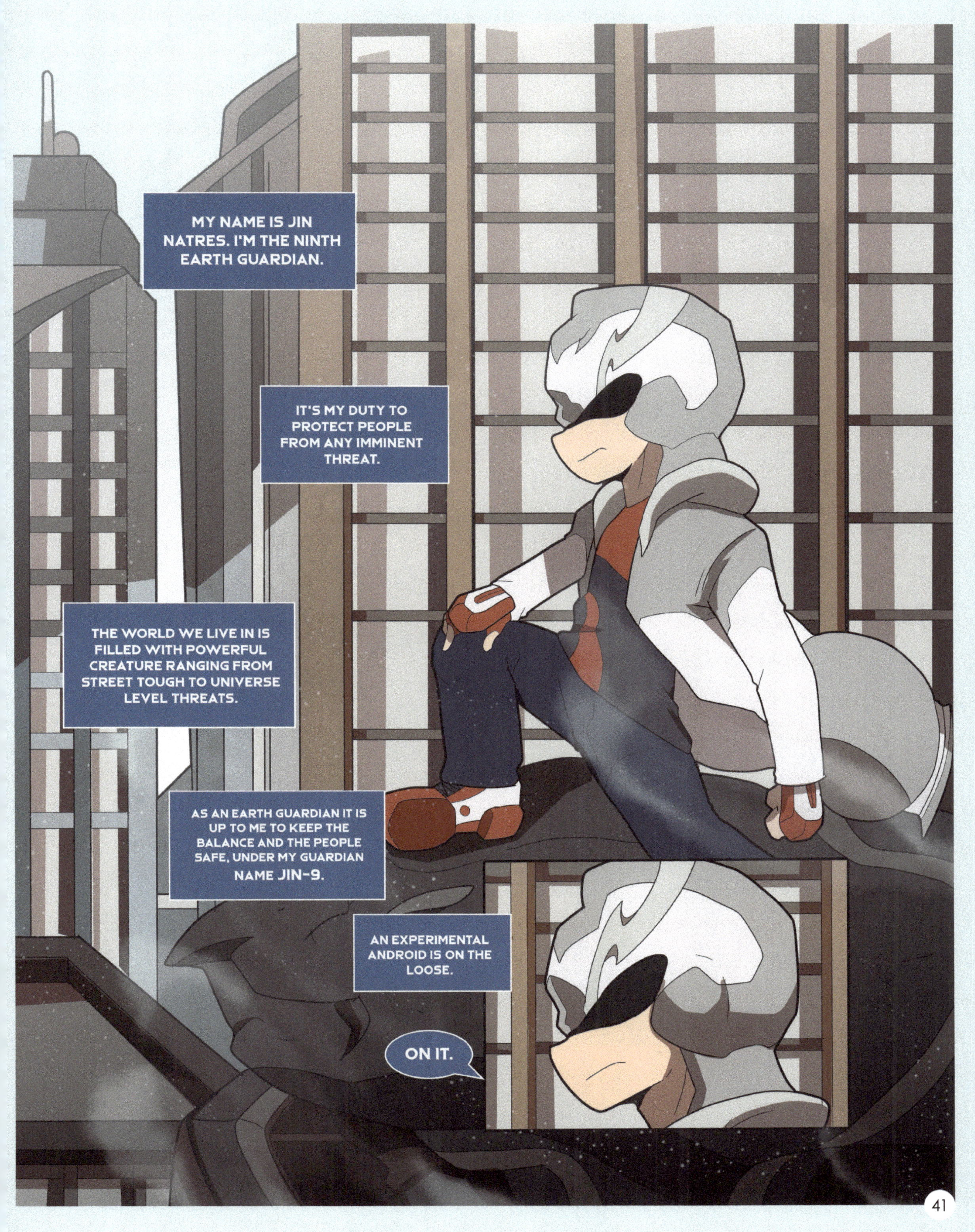
MY NAME IS JIN NATRES. I'M THE NINTH EARTH GUARDIAN.
IT'S MY DUTY TO PROTECT PEOPLE FROM ANY IMMINENT THREAT.
THE WORLD WE LIVE IN IS FILLED WITH POWERFUL CREATURE RANGING FROM STREET TOUGH TO UNIVERSE LEVEL THREATS.
AS AN EARTH GUARDIAN IT IS UP TO ME TO KEEP THE BALANCE AND THE PEOPLE SAFE, UNDER MY GUARDIAN NAME JIN-9.
AN EXPERIMENTAL ANDROID IS ON THE LOOSE.
ON IT.

NEED A HAND, GWEN?
NO NEED, I GOT THIS.

THAT'S MY OLDER SISTER, GWEN NATRES, SHE'S AN EVOLVED XZAPIAN.
A HUMAN BORN WITH NATURAL GENETICS MODIFICATION OR EVO POWER,
ALLOWING HER TO HAVE INCREDIBLE ABILITIES BASED ON HOW MUCH SHE CAN CONTROL HER EVO POWER.
SHE RUNS AN ORGANIZATION ALONGSIDE HER PARTNERS TO TRAIN YOUNG KIDS STRUGGLING TO CONTROL THEIR EVO POWER.

HUH?
NGH!

STAY BACK!
HE GETS STRONGER THE LONGER HE FIGHTS.

GAH!
HRRAAAAAGGGGHHH!

ILLUSION
TAKEDOWN!

YEAH.

YOU OKAY?

I'M SURPRISED HOW MUCH YOU'VE GROWN IN THE LAST COUPLE OF WEEKS.
IT'S ONLY DUE TO THE IMMENSE POWER STORED INSIDE
I'M ONLY GROWING BECAUSE OF IT.

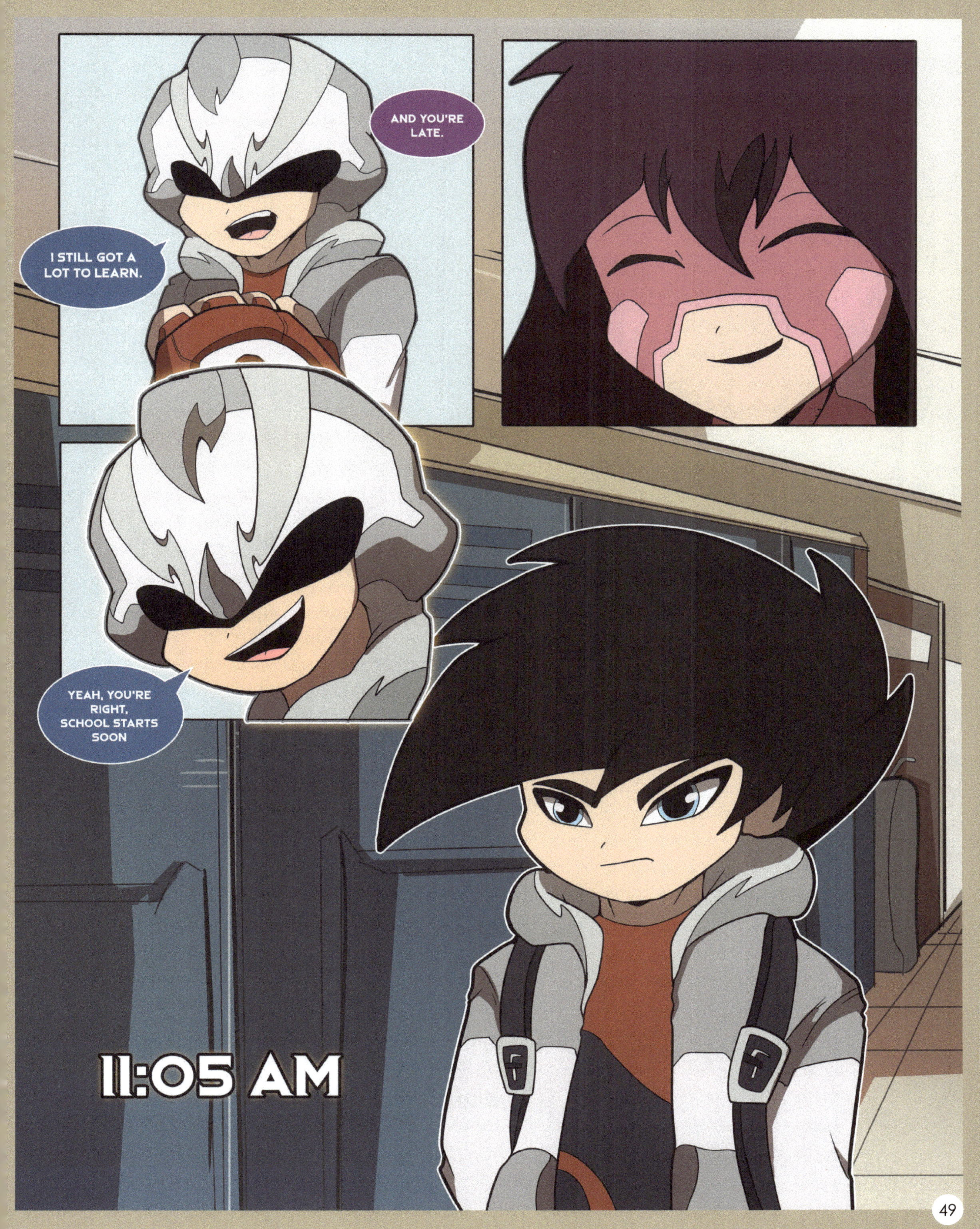

AND YOU'RE LATE.
I STILL GOT A LOT TO LEARN.
YEAH, YOU'RE RIGHT, SCHOOL STARTS SOON
11:05 AM

LOOK AT HIM, GO.
THAT COWL IS SO COOL, MY GOD HE'S SO DREAMY.
GEE.... WHAT'S UP WITH FANGIRLS.
ANOTHER BORING DAY TO START THE WEEK OFF, CAN'T WAIT FOR IT.
ALRIGHT, CLASS, BEFORE WE START, LET'S WELCOME OUR NEW CLASSMATE.

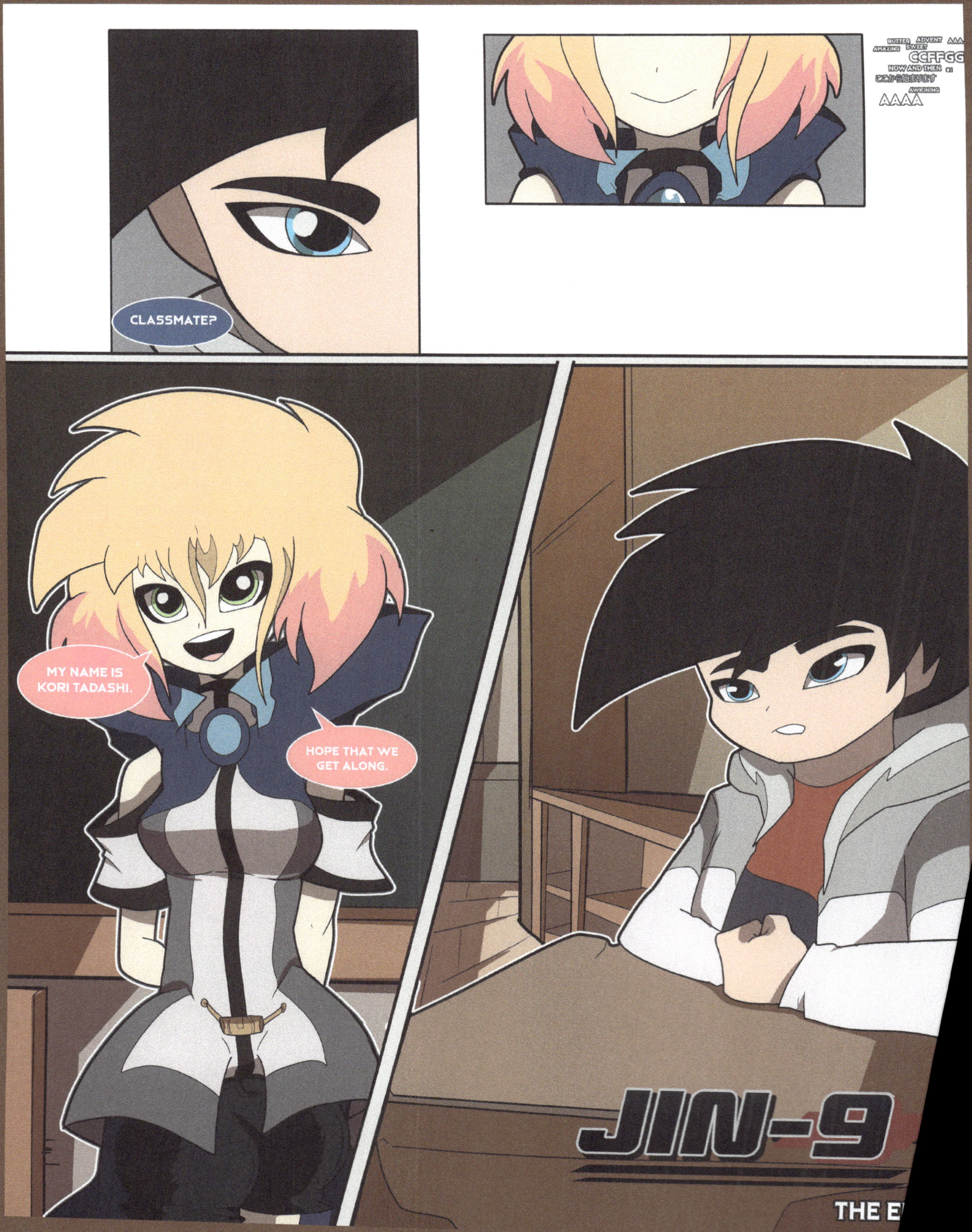

JIN-9

THE E

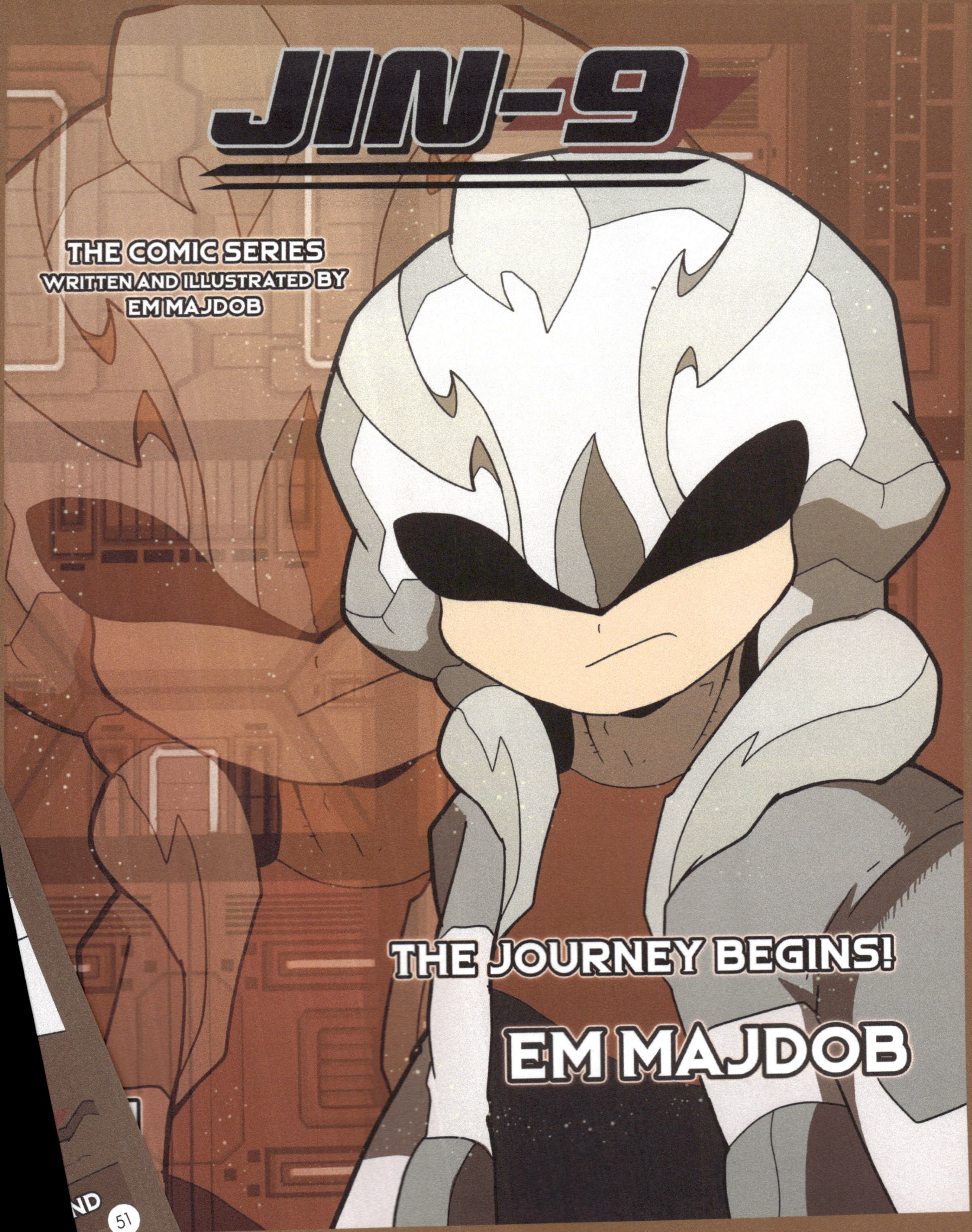

JIN-9
THE COMIC SERIES
WRITTEN AND ILLUSTRATED BY
EM MAJDOB
THE JOURNEY BEGINS!
EM MAJDOB

PG01

CONCEPT ART

AUTHOR'S NOTES

JIN-9 WAS THE FIRST CHARACTER I'VE EVER CREATED
SINCE I WAS ELEVEN YEARS OLD.

PG02

CONCEPT ART

I WANTED TO CREATE AN INNOCENT ADORABLY-CHARMING ENERGETIC YOUNG BOY, WHO'S ALSO THE MOST OVERPOWERED 12 YEARS KID

YOU'LL EVER SEE, AND HE DISPLAYS THAT IN THE MOST INNOCENT WAY POSSIBLE TO HIS MASSIVE MENACING LOOKING OPPONENTS.

GIRLS AND ROBOTS

GIRLS AND ROBOTS

AERO
EM MAJDOB
1

HAHAHA!
HAHAHA!
HA-HA! WE RACKED A NEW RECORD, BOYS! WE'RE SOON HEADING OUR WAY TO A DRUG-DEALING EMPIRE.
DON'T BE AN IDIOT
FOR ALL IT"S WORTH, THE MONEY ONLY SATISFIES OUR CREWS, THERE AIN"T GONNA BE ANY LEFTOVERS.

HOW ABOUT I TAKE A SHOT AT YOU?
GOLD AMULETS, SKIN-TIGHT PANTS THAT BARELY FITS YOUR ASS, A STEREOTYPICAL GANG BOOZE OVER HERE.
NOW WE CAN DO THIS THE EASY WAY OR THE HARD WAY.
BUT I CAN FORGIVE YOUR SORRY ASS IF YOU DO ONE THING.
BOW DOWN TO ME.

WHO DO YA
THINK YOU
ARE!

BLAST HIS
BUTT OFF!

HARD WAY
IT IS.

SNAP!

PLEASE! DON'T KILL ME!
I-I'LL PAY ANYTHING! ANY AMOUNT YOU WANT!
BOW DOWN TO ME.
YES.

HA-HA! PATHETIC! WITH THIS LEVEL OF DIGNITY, I CAN STRIP YOUR CLOTHES AND THROW IN THE STREET!
BUT I AM A MERCIFUL MAN.
GET LOST!

PG01

CONCEPT ART

THIS IS A REJECTED SUBMISSION TO IMAGE COMICS THAT NEVER SAW THE LIGHT OF DAY.

IT'S ABOUT A POWERFUL MASKED CRUSADER NAMED AERO. WHAT'S INTERESTING ABOUT HIM FOR ME IS HOW POWERFUL HE IS IN EVERY SCENE HE'S IN. HE'S ALWAYS IN CONTROL.

AN IMMOVABLE OBJECT AND HE'S A LOOSE CANNON YOU'LL NEVER KNOW WHAT HE DOES NEXT AND MOST IMPORTANTLY WE DON'T ANYTHING ABOUT HIM

EXCEPT HIS NAME, HIS APPEARANCE AND HIS POWERS

PG02

CONCEPT ART

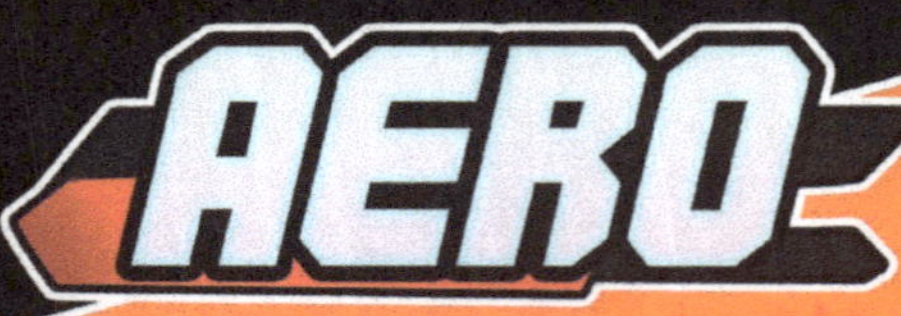

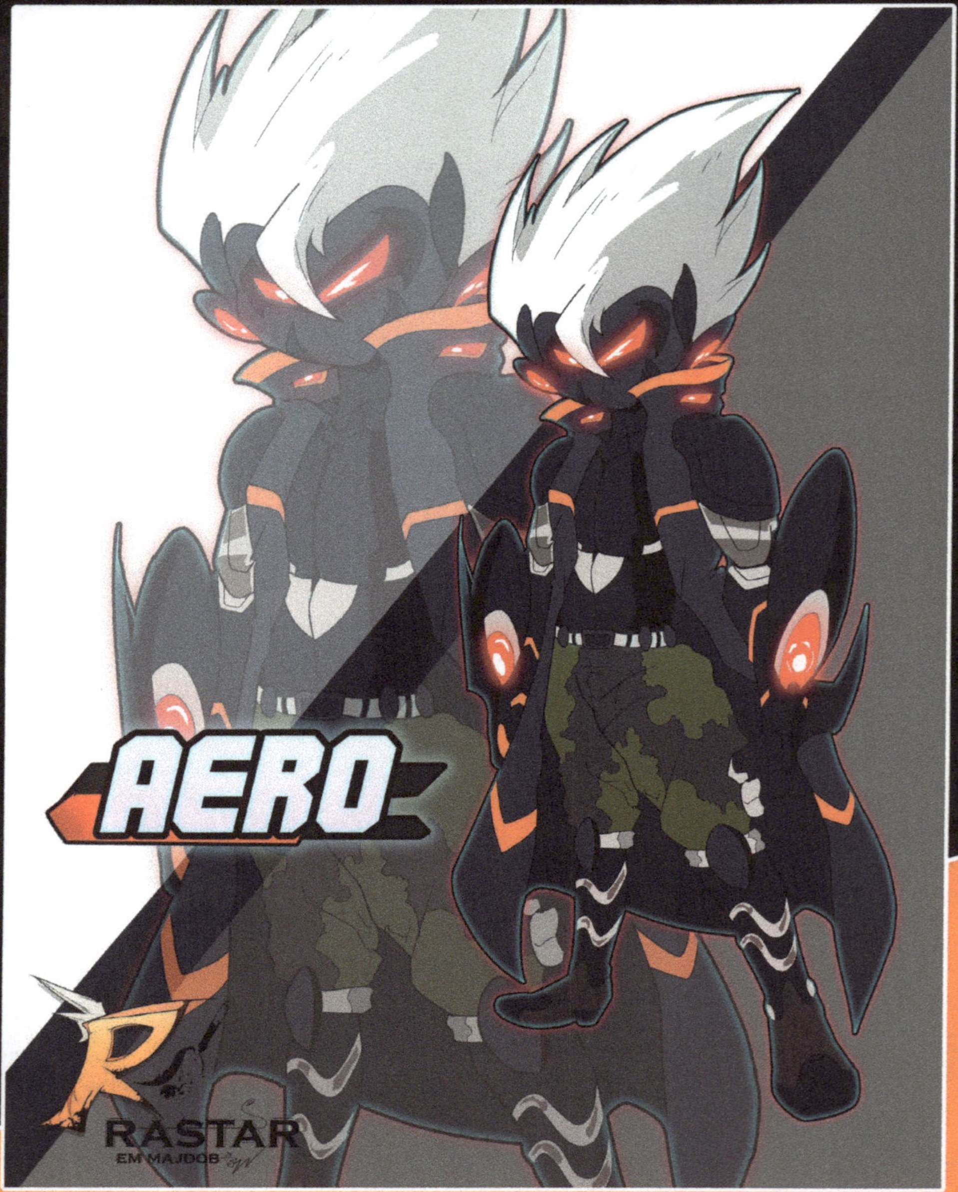

AERO

HERE'S AN OLD DRAWING I DID OF AERO IN 2019 AND HERE'S THE SAME IMAGE

BUT WITH A HIGHER COLORING SKILL.

THIS PROVES THAT WHILE THE DRAWING ASPECT IS ESSENTIAL THE COLORING SKILL WOULD MAKE OR BREAK YOUR ART.

PG03

CONCEPT ART

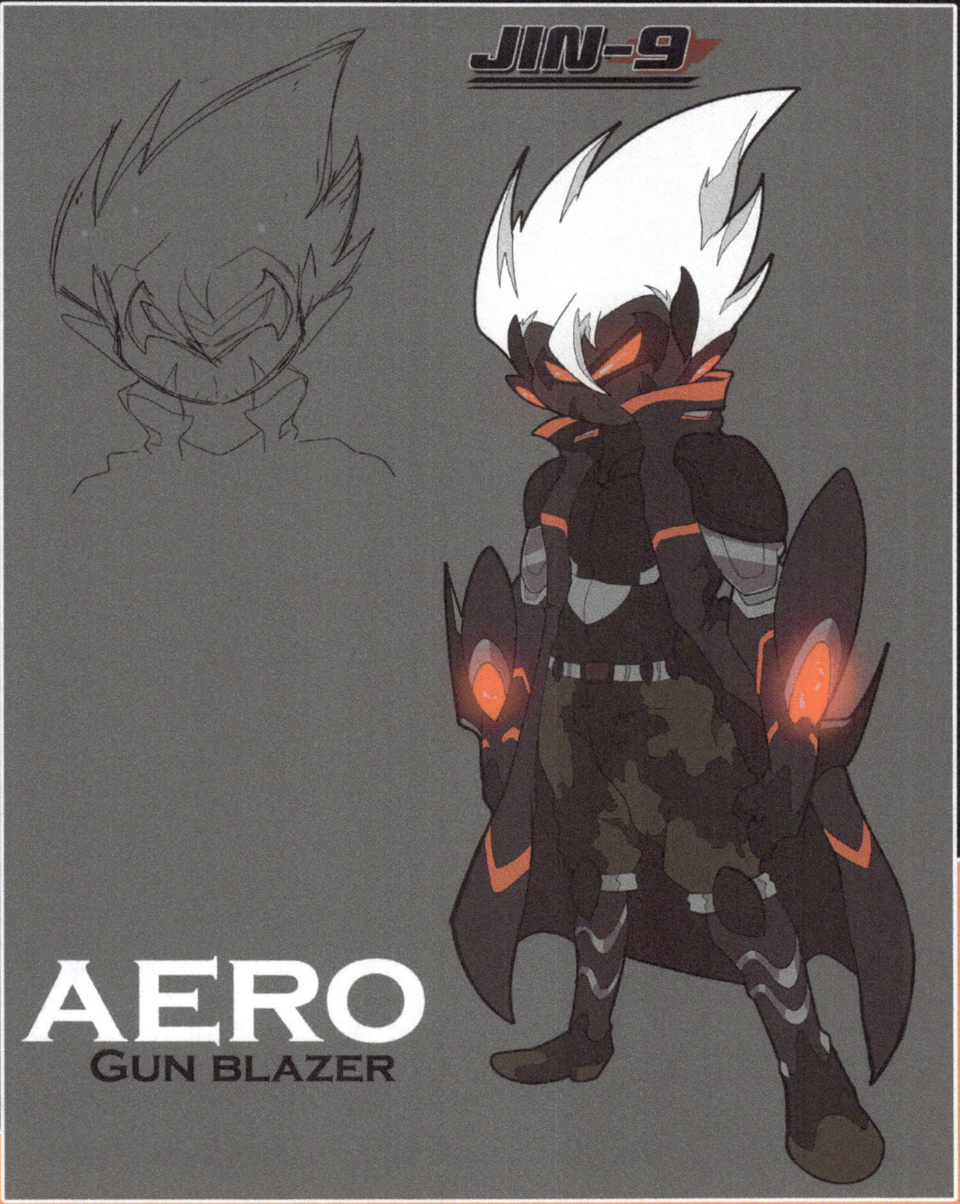
JIN-9
AERO
GUN BLAZER

AERO

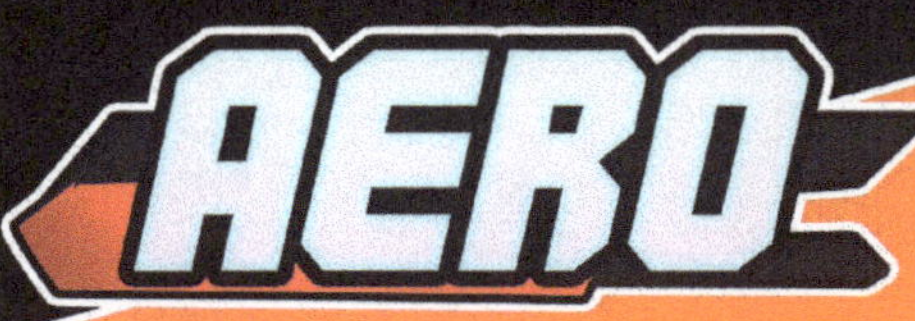

HERE'S AN OLD DRAWING I DID OF AERO IN 2019 AND HERE'S THE SAME IMAGE

BUT WITH A HIGHER COLORING SKILL.

THIS PROVES THAT WHILE THE DRAWING ASPECT IS ESSENTIAL THE COLORING SKILL WOULD MAKE OR BREAK YOUR ART.

STOMP
STOMP
STOMP
AAAAAGGGHH!
SWOOSH
PGOZ
Anicomic
WHAAAT THE FUCK!!!

PG01

Anicomic

DONT MESS WITH THE DRAGON CLAN

JIN-9

JIN-9
THE COMIC SERIES
WRITTEN AND ILLUSTRATED BY
EM MAJDOB
THE JOURNEY BEGINS!
EM MAJDOB
#1

CLASSMATE?

BUTTER ADVENT AAA
AMAZING SWEET
CCFFGG
NOW AND THEN et
ここから始まります
AWAKENING
AAAA

MY NAME IS KORI TADASHI.
HOPE THAT WE GET ALONG.
JIN-9

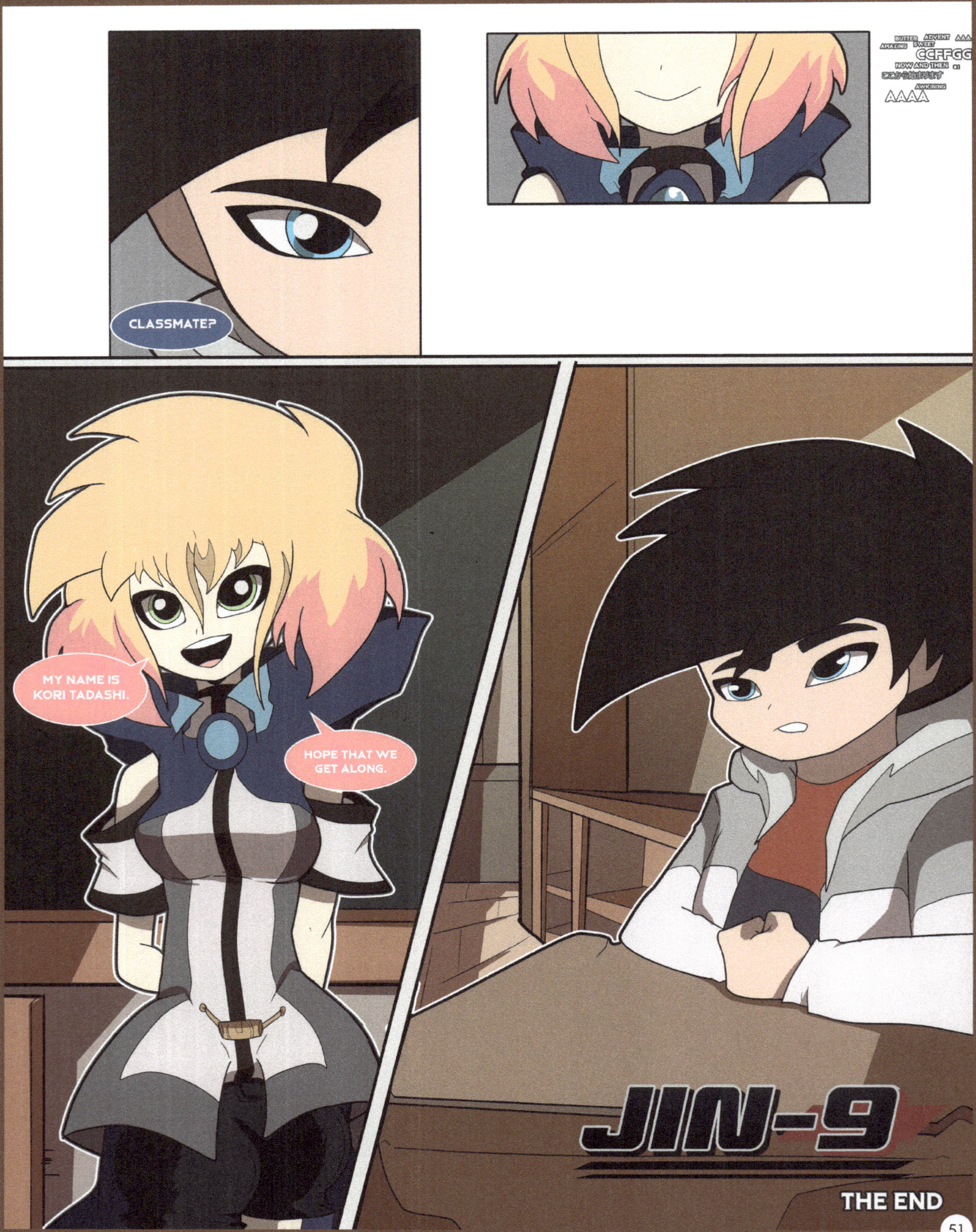

THE END

DON'T PANIC! IT'S JUST PART OF THEIR TRICKS!
PG03
ANiCOMiC

WE CAN TAKE"EM!!
AAAAAGGGHH!

AAAAAGGGHH!
CRACK
CRACK
WHOOOOSH
HELP!
RAGE OF THE ELEMENTS
PG04
Anicomic

KRAAKKOOOM
PG05
Anicomic
LIGHTINING
STRIKE

PG06
Anicomic

NEVER MESS WITH DRAGON SHINOBI CLAN